THE CASE
Walkabout Clock

THE CASE OF THE Walkabout Clock

DUNCAN BALL

ILLUSTRATED BY MARK DAVID

To Sam,
all the best,

Angus&Robertson
An imprint of HarperCollins*Publishers*

To Cass and Robin – Mark

Angus&Robertson
An imprint of HarperCollins*Publishers*, Australia

First published in Australia in 1994
Reprinted in 1998
by HarperCollins*Publishers* Pty Limited
ACN 009 913 517
A member of the HarperCollins*Publishers* (Australia) Pty Limited Group
http://www.harpercollins.com.au

HarperCollins*Publishers*
25 Ryde Road, Pymble, Sydney, NSW 2073, Australia
31 View Road, Glenfield, Auckland 10, New Zealand
77-85 Fulham Palace Road, London W6 8JB, United Kingdom
Hazelton Lanes, 55 Avenue Road, Suite 2900, Toronto, Ontario M5R 3L2
and 1995 Markham Road, Scarborough, Ontario M1B 5M8, Canada
10 East 53rd Street, New York NY 10032, USA

National Library of Australia Cataloguing-in-Publication data:

Ball, Duncan, 1941– .
The case of the walkabout clock.
ISBN 0 207 18297 3.
I. David, Mark. II. Title. (Series: Skinny books)
A823.3

Printed in Australia by McPherson's Printing Group on 80gsm Econoprint

7 6 5 4 3 2
01 00 99 98

'Well kids,' Mrs Wagner said,
'have you seen the big surprise?'

Mrs Wagner struggled against the wind to close the door. She was holding a handful of mail.

They found it hanging on the wall.

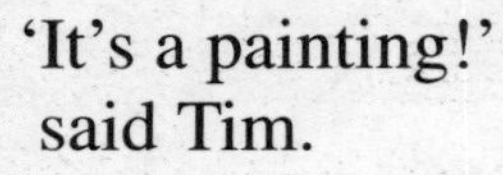

'It's a painting!'
said Tim.

'It's really a clock,'
his mother said.
'Have a closer look.'

In the middle of the painting of a town was a church.

And on the church was a steeple.

And on the steeple was a clock — a real clock with hands that moved. Just then the clock struck four.

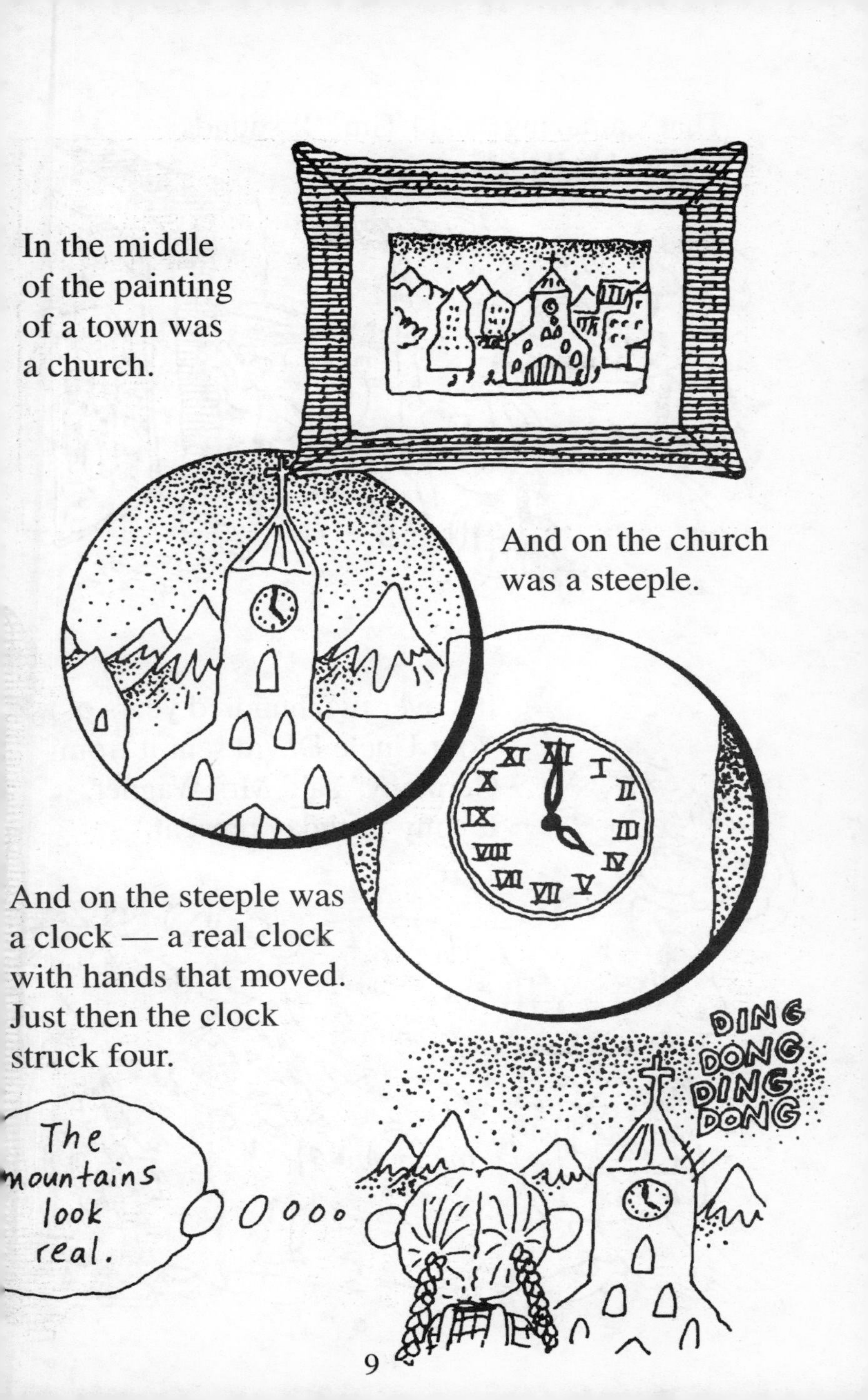

The mountains look real.
DING DONG DING DONG

'That's amazing!' said Tim. 'It sounds like real bells!'

'It's over two hundred years old. Your Uncle David sent it from Germany,' said Mrs Wagner. 'It's my birthday present.'

Wasn't that sweet of him?
He must miss you.

‘It’s probably worth a fortune,’ Tim said. ‘You could sell it and get a lot of money.’

‘Tim! I couldn’t possibly sell my birthday present. It’s true that I need the money. Look at all these bills,’ Mrs Wagner said.

She looked at the mail. ‘There’s only one — right in the middle — that isn’t a bill.’

I was only kidding about selling it.
I wonder what it is.

'I'll open it,'
Anna said,
ripping open
the envelope.

'Look! It's a
family ticket
to *Rossini's*
Super Circus!
No letter,
just the ticket.'

'It's for tonight —
at seven!'
said Tim.

‘I wonder who it’s from,’ Mrs Wagner said.

‘Can we go?’ Tim pleaded. ‘Please?’

‘Maybe the circus sent it to me because I’m a journalist,’ Mrs Wagner decided. ‘They’ll want me to write a story about it for the newspaper.’

It was so windy that the circus workers had trouble putting up the tent.

Finally, the wind stopped. Everyone then went in to see the show.

Fantastic!
There were lions and tigers and elephants and acrobats and a very funny clown act. Tim and Anna laughed till their stomachs hurt.

When it was over, Mrs Wagner went to see the circus owner, Mr Rossini. She was ready to take notes for her article.

She told him how much they had enjoyed the circus. 'I'm glad you liked it,' he said, 'but what's this about a free ticket? I didn't send you a ticket.'

Mrs Wagner showed him her ticket.

'Very strange,' he said. 'Someone else must have bought it and sent it to you. It has the price on it. Free tickets never have a price on them.'

'I wonder who sent it?' Mrs Wagner mused. 'It was very nice of them, whoever they were.'

When they got home they found the front door wide open. Someone had broken the lock. Tim and Anna raced to the lounge room.

'The clock's gone walkabout!' Tim cried.

'What do you mean?'
asked Mrs Wagner.

'It's been stolen!' said Anna. 'Look!'

Sure enough, there was a blank space on the wall where the clock had been.

'The ticket wasn't such a nice gift,' said Anna.
'Someone must have sent it to get us out of the house so they could break in.'
'Did anyone know you had the clock?' asked Tim.

'I only told Narelle Sullivan,' Mrs Wagner said.

Not Mrs Sullivan!
I'm afraid so.

'Then everyone must have known,' Tim sighed. 'She's the biggest gossip in town!'

'Yes, you're right,' Mrs Wagner said. 'Oh, well, I guess we'd better ring the police.'

The next morning
Sergeant McNabbem came to investigate.

'My brother said
it was probably
the only one in
Australia,' said
Mrs Wagner.

I don't suppose we'll ever get the clock back?
Don't you worry.
Any clues?

'I know who might have done it,' Sergeant McNabbem said. 'Remember Bluey Blake, the burglar? The one with the big hat? Well, he's out of jail again.'

'I interviewed him for the newspaper last week,' Mrs Wagner said. 'He said he won't break the law ever again. He says he's straight now.'

'That bloke's about as straight as a snake.
I'll get him down to the cop shop and ask a few questions.
Want to come along?'
I'd love to come along.
Let's go.

Once their mother and the policeman had gone, Anna said to Tim, 'This is a good little mystery. Let's see if we can solve it.'
'First let's find the envelope that the ticket came in, Anna. That might give us a clue about who sent it.'
Where would Mum have put it?
The wastepaper basket.

They found the envelope
in the wastepaper basket.
This is it!
Yeah, look! Someone wrote "Rossini's Super Circus" on the back.

'Hey! There's no stamp,' Tim said.
'It couldn't have come through the post office.
The burglar must have dropped it in our mailbox himself!'
'Or herself,' added Anna.
Could that be?
I wonder.

'No,' said Anna.
'I think Mr Adams, the postman, delivered it.
You've missed a clue. Remember what Mum said when she was going through the letters?'
Yes!

'Of course! She said that the one with the ticket was in the *middle* of the stack,' he said.

'That means it was put in the mailbox with the other letters.'

Exactly,' said Anna.
f it was put in the
nailbox before or
after the postman
came, it would have
been on the top or
on the bottom —
not in the middle!

Look! There's Mr Adams
now. Let's see if we can
get more clues from him.'

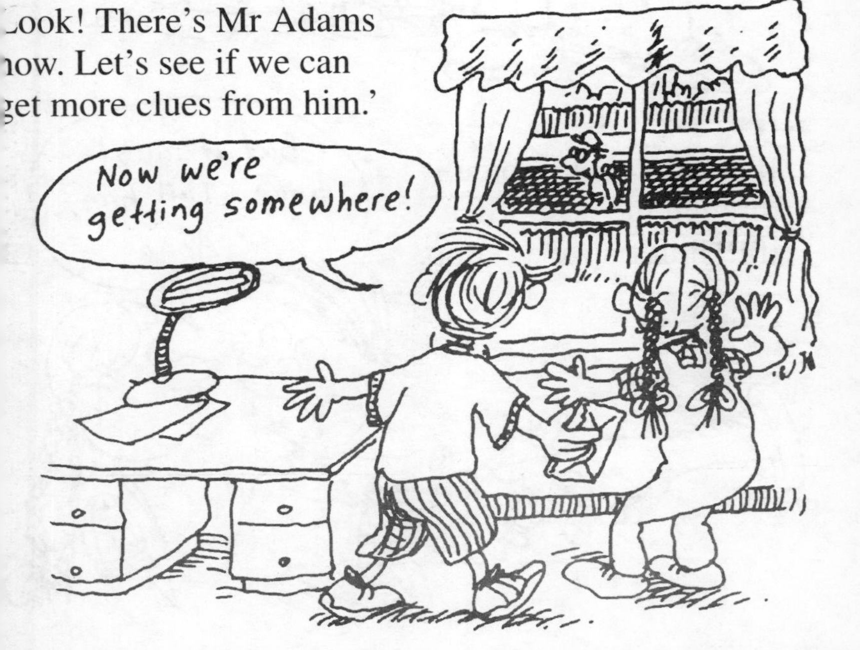
Now we're getting somewhere!

'Very strange,' the postman said. 'But I'm sure I didn't deliver it.

It couldn't have come through the post office if it didn't have a stamp.'

But it must have. Tell him, Anna.

'It was in the middle of all the letters that came yesterday,' Anna said. 'You must have delivered it.'

Let's see if I can remember...
There was a lock on the mailbox. No one could have put it in the middle of the stack except you.
Good point.

'Maybe someone dropped it in my pack before I came here.

With these backpacks all someone has to do is sneak up behind and drop it in.

There was a strange man over on Jacaranda Street.

Maybe he put it in my pack.

But what's this all about?'

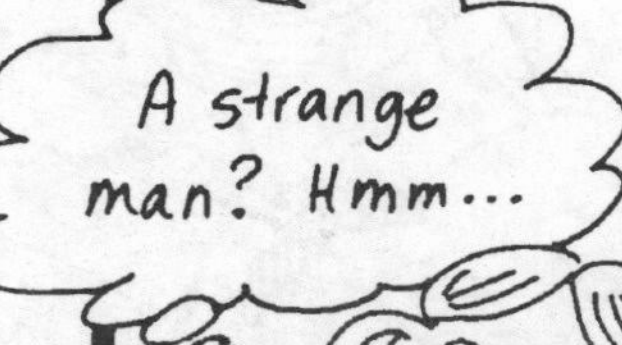
A strange man? Hmm...

'There was a free family ticket to the circus in this envelope,' Anna said. 'When we went out, someone broke into the house and stole Mum's clock. We're looking for clues.'

A missing clock?
Yes. I'm afraid it's gone walkabout.
That's too bad.

'The burglary must have happened between seven o'clock and nine o'clock last night,' Tim said.

'Between seven and nine, you say?' said Mr Adams. 'Well, here's a clue for you: the burglar wasn't a basketball fan.'

'Why do you say that?' asked Tim.

'Because the *Wildcats* were playing the *Kings*. It was on TV. It was a great game.'

‘What time were you in Jacaranda Street yesterday?’ Tim said.

Mr Adams got out a round watch and looked at it. ‘Let’s see, it’s now ten o’clock,’ he said. ‘I was probably on Jacaranda Street at about nine-thirty-five.’

'And that strange man?'
Anna asked.
'Do you know who he is?'

Can you tell us what he looked like?
This town is small enough. We should be able to find the thief.

'I saw a picture of him in the newspaper.
He always wears a big wide hat.'

'Aha!' said Anna.
'I think we've found
the burglar.'
He must
mean Bluey Blake.

'Me, too,' said Tim. 'Would you mind coming with us to tell the police, Mr Adams?'

'I'd be happy to,' Mr Adams said.

I'm always glad to help.

At the police station, Bluey Blake was yelling at Sergeant McNabbem and Mrs Wagner.

'Oh, no you don't, you two!' Bluey screamed. 'You're not going to pin this rap on me!'

'Excuse me, Sergeant McNabbem,' Anna said. 'Mr Adams, the postie, has some information.'

'I think the circus ticket came from Mr Blake,' Mr Adams said. 'I was in his street before I got to the Wagner's house. I think he dropped the envelope in my pack. I remember him because of that hat.'

'Me? I don't know what you're talking about, stamp-head!' Bluey Blake yelled.

I never done it!

'I told you I was at home watching TV last night. Search my house if you want to You won't find any old clocks there.'

'Okay, smart guy,'
Sergeant McNabbem said.
'What were you watching
on TV between seven
and nine o'clock?'

'How should I know?'
said Bluey Blake. 'I can't
remember what I watched.'

What do you think I am? A human computer?
And I believed him when he said he was going to go straight.

'Well, you can tell
that to the magistrate.
I'm going to charge you
with stealing that clock,'
Sergeant McNabbem said.

'Excuse me, Sergeant,' Anna interrupted,
'but I don't believe Mr Blake stole the clock.'

'I don't think so either,' Tim said. 'Mr Adams is the real burglar.'

'Me?' Mr Adams said. 'I've never stolen anything in my life!'

'Tim! That's a terrible thing
to say!' cried Mrs Wagner.
But it's true.
'Tell them, Anna,'
said Tim.
You'd better explain.

‘Okay,’ said Anna. ‘Whoever stole the clock wasn’t going to sell it. Every antique shop and every clock collector in Australia would know it was stolen.’

'They'd be on
the lookout for it,'
Anna continued.
'So it was probably
taken by someone
who wants to keep it.
Someone who knows about clocks.'
'You like old clocks,
don't you,
Mr Adams?'
Tim asked.

'They're okay,' Mr Adams said. 'So what?'

'Could you show us that pocket watch of yours?' Tim asked. 'It looks like an antique to me. Only someone who really liked old clocks would carry a pocket watch.'

That bloke's a real drop kick.
I haven't seen one of those for donkey's years.

‘That doesn’t prove anything,’ Mr Adams said, showing it to them. ‘I was watching the basketball game last night.

Mr Blake here doesn’t even remember what he watched.’

'Lots of people
forget what they see
on TV,' said Anna.
'That's not unusual.
What is unusual is
that you told us
exactly what you
were watching —
for no reason.'
'You told us about
the basketball game
so we wouldn't
suspect you,'
said Tim.
'That's when
I started to
suspect you.'

'And I suspected you when you said you didn't deliver the ticket,' Anna said.
You must have delivered it.
'Then you made up the excuse about Mr Blake dropping it in your pack,' said Tim.
It couldn't have been anyone else.

'Don't postmen sort out their mail before they leave the post office?' asked Anna. 'It's all in bunches with rubber bands around it. If there was a loose letter with no stamps in your pack, you would have noticed it.'

‘Then you told a really big lie,’ said Tim.
‘We knew you had something
to hide, didn’t we Anna?’

'Yes,' said Anna.
'The wind gave you away.'

'What does the wind
have to do with
anything?' asked
Sergeant McNabbem.

'Mr Adams said he saw Mr Blake on the street,' said Anna. 'He said he was wearing that big wide hat. But he couldn't have been. It was too windy. The hat would have blown off.'
Yep! I can't wear this hat on a windy day.
Pretty smart for a kid.

'That's right,' said Tim.
'Search Mr Adams' house
and you'll find
Mum's clock.'

Well, Mr Adams?
I've got to hand it to those kids.

'All right,' Mr Adams sighed. 'You're right. I just had to have that clock for my collection. It's so beautiful! They only made them between 1775 and 1793 in one city in Germany. I heard Mrs Sullivan blabbing about it and knew I had to have it. So I bought the ticket and put it in your mailbox. I'm sorry.'

'Yeah, well, you won't get any sympathy from me,' Bluey Blake muttered.

Later that day, the clock was back in the Wagner's house.

'Thanks, kids,' Mrs Wagner said. 'You're a clever pair of detectives.'

'The evidence was all there,' said Anna. 'All we had to do was use our heads without losing our heads.'